TV Time

T0333161

Written by Jillian Powell

Illustrated by Andrea Castro Naranjo

Collins

Who's in this story?

Listen and say

Download the audio at www.collins.co.uk/839765

Mum

Grandpa

Max

🎧 Max is playing a game on his tablet. Lucy is reading a book on her tablet.

Mum is looking at her computer.
Dad is cooking, and reading on
his phone.

Max sees Grandpa in the living room.

Grandpa is sitting in the armchair.
He's watching television.

Grandpa says, "Hello, Max. This is funny. Come and see."

Max says, "I'm playing a game on my tablet."

Max says, "Look. It's a football game. It's great!"

Max says, "You try, Grandpa."

Grandpa says, "It's good, but the TV is good, too."

Grandpa says, "Listen, Max. I can see a young me and my family watching our old TV."

"We love the television. It's funny."

"We watch football. It's a great game! My mum's very happy."

"One night, my brother and I are sleeping. Dad gets us."

"We see men on the moon!"

"One day, there's a new television. The pictures are colour, not black and white! Me, my mum, my dad and my brother – watching TV."

Wow!

Grandpa tells Max lots of stories about TV.

Max says, "Let's watch TV with Grandpa!"

Max says, "You're right. This is good!"

Picture dictionary

Listen and repeat

computer

phone

picture

tablet

television (TV)

watch

1 Look and order the story

2 Listen and say

Collins

Published by Collins
An imprint of HarperCollins*Publishers*
Westerhill Road
Bishopbriggs
Glasgow
G64 2QT

HarperCollins*Publishers*
1st Floor, Watermarque Building
Ringsend Road
Dublin 4
Ireland

William Collins' dream of knowledge for all began with the publication of his first book in 1819.

A self-educated mill worker, he not only enriched millions of lives, but also founded a flourishing publishing house. Today, staying true to this spirit, Collins books are packed with inspiration, innovation and practical expertise. They place you at the centre of a world of possibility and give you exactly what you need to explore it.

10 9 8 7 6 5 4 3 2

ISBN 978-0-00-839765-4

Collins® and COBUILD® are registered trademarks of HarperCollins*Publishers* Limited

www.collins.co.uk/elt

British Library Cataloguing in Publication Data

A catalogue record for this publication is available from the British Library.

Author: Jillian Powell
Illustrator: Andrea Castro Naranjo (Beehive)
Series editor: Rebecca Adlard
Publishing manager: Lisa Todd
Product managers: Jennifer Hall and Caroline Green
In-house editor: Alma Puts Keren
Project manager: Emily Hooton
Editor: Emma Wilkinson
Proofreaders: Natalie Murray and Michael Lamb
Cover designer: Kevin Robbins
Typesetter: 2Hoots Publishing Services Ltd
Audio produced by id audio, London
Reading guide author: Emma Wilkinson
Production controller: Rachel Weaver
Printed and bound by: GPS Group, Slovenia

MIX
Paper from
responsible sources
FSC™ C007454

This book is produced from independently certified FSC™ paper to ensure responsible forest management.

For more information visit: **www.harpercollins.co.uk/green**

Download the audio for this book and a reading guide for parents and teachers at www.collins.co.uk/839765